PHONICS CHAPTER BOOK

Tall in the Saddle

by Argentina Palacios
Illustrated by Deborah DeSaix

Scholastic Inc.
New York Toronto London Auckland Sydney
Mexico City New Delhi Hong Kong

No part of this publication may be reproduced in whole or in part, or stored in a retrieval system, or transmitted in any form or by any means, electronic, mechanical, photocopying, recording, or otherwise, without written permission of the publisher. For information regarding permission, write to Scholastic Inc., Instructional Publishing Group, 555 Broadway, New York, NY 10012.

ISBN 0-439-04694-7

12 11 10 9 8 7 6 5   5 6 7 8 9/0
Printed in the U.S.A.   23
First Scholastic printing, January 1999

Dear Teacher/Family Member,

Scholastic Phonics Chapter Books provide early readers with interesting stories in easy-to-manage chapters. The books in this series are controlled for sounds and common sight words. Once sounds and sight words have been introduced, they are repeated frequently to give children lots of reading practice and to build children's confidence. When children experience success in reading, they want to read more, and when they read more, they become better readers.

Phonics instruction teaches children the way words work and gives them the strategies they need to become fluent, independent readers. However, phonics can only be effective when reading is meaningful and children have the opportunity to read many different kinds of books. Scholastic Phonics Chapter Books cover many curricular areas and genres. They are carefully designed to help build good readers, but more importantly, to inspire children to love reading.

Contents

1 The Riders Are Ready

It was David's birthday, and for a treat his Mom and Dad were taking him and his brother Sam to a riding stable.

First they had lunch in the main building. Everyone had a piece of Mom's super frozen banana layer cake.

Peter Fox, the owner of the stable, had a piece, too. Then he asked, "Are the riders ready? Let's hit the trail."

David and Sam put on riding helmets, got on their horses, and looked like riders.

The horses followed each other along a winding trail. Peter led the group. He showed them a nest where a robin sat on her eggs. He pointed out the green clover and pink tulips that lined the trail.

The riders had the best time! At the end of the day, Peter said, "Come back soon."

After that, whenever David had time, he would visit the stable. He liked to see the workers feed and brush the horses and the riders get ready.

One day, Peter told David about his plans. "I want to make the stable more beautiful. I'm going to build some flower boxes and fill them with tulips. I'll build some benches, too. I was hoping you might help with the horses while I'm doing the building."

"Super! I would love that," said David, "but you will have to ask my mom."

Peter called David's mom. He said, "Jill works at the stable. David will work with her. She will be the teacher and David will be her student."

David's mom thought for a moment. Then she said that was fine.

The next day, Peter gave David a book filled with blank pieces of paper. "You can keep a log about the things you do here," he said.

David couldn't wait to begin.

2 A Super Student

"Hi!" Jill greeted David on his first day. She held a small basin in her hand. "Let's begin," she said. "Major, that brown-and-white horse, needs a bath."

Jill handed David a blue hose. She put soap from the basin on Major. Then she asked David to spray water on the horse.

Major looked shiny and clean when the job was done!

David's Log   May 12

Today I helped give Major a bath. Major is a bit too big for a tub, so we used a hose. This was more messy than it sounds! Major didn't seem to mind, but I think I will start wearing boots to the stable!

"The horses need fresh food and water every day," Jill said to David on his next visit. "Let's begin with Pilot."

Jill filled Pilot's bucket with food from a big can with a blue label. Then she filled a pan with fresh water.

After Pilot was fed, Jill asked David to give Major his food and water.

MAJOR

PILOT

"It's good to call a horse by its name," Jill said. "Get in the habit of patting each horse and talking to it. That way the horse will get to know your voice and will relax and feel safe with you."

David's Log   May 13
You can talk to horses to make them happy and relaxed. Today I told Pilot a funny story about the time we were at Clover Lake and a spider dropped from Mom's hat onto her nose. Pilot looked like he was smiling. I think he liked it!

FEED

David began each visit by walking along the stalls and reading the names of the horses. Besides Pilot and Major, there were Clover, Sweet Music, Tulip, and Raven.

"It's time to learn how to walk a horse," said Jill. "Let's begin with Raven. She's the one who minds me best."

"Always walk on the left side of a horse," Jill said. "Watch how I lead her. Your right hand leads the horse. Your left hand holds the rope. Hold the rope high, away from the ground."

Jill let David walk Raven. He didn't trip over the rope once.

David's Log   May 14

Jill is a super teacher. (She said I was a good student, too.) I learned how to walk a horse today. Sometimes I wish I could have a horse of my own. Maybe I'd name him Tall Rider.

David was a very good pupil. He learned something new on each visit.

"The horses need to be brushed," Jill said to him one morning.

Jill opened a big blue box and took out brushes and combs. "When you brush a horse, you have to get close," Jill said. "You want the horse to relax."

Jill began brushing Pilot. "Always begin by brushing the near side—that's the left side of the horse," she said.

Then she moved to the other side. "Next, you brush the off side—that's the right side of the horse."

Jill brushed Pilot's tail, holding it up in one hand as she pulled the blue comb through it. The mane was the last part to be brushed. David got to do that.

David's Log   May 20
Today I learned how to brush a horse.
We began with Pilot. He sure didn't seem
to mind. Talk about relaxed! He leaned
against the brush until I thought he was
going to fall right over!

One time, a man named Jason came by to take care of the horses' feet. He had a small wagon filled with nails and files and metal horseshoes. Jason filed the horses' hoofs and put on the horseshoes.

"Doesn't it hurt when you pound those nails into their feet?" David asked.

"Not if you do it right," Jason said.

After he checked the horseshoes, Jason asked Jill and David to make sure there were no nails left on the ground.

David's Log   May 28

I keep thinking about those nails in Jason's wagon. They were big! Raven and Tulip didn't seem to mind when they got their new horseshoes. I'm going to bring them both a carrot the next time I visit.

3 ⭐ Acorn

"Do you want another horse?" a man asked Peter one morning. The man pointed to a horse in his van. The horse was a soft brown color just like an acorn.

"I'd like one," Peter said, "but now is not a good time."

David was watching the horse. He walked over to Peter and the man. "Wait!" he said, "I want that horse!"

"Are you sure? Do you even know if your mom and dad would let you?" the man asked.

David didn't know. He could just hope that they would think it over and say yes.

"Can I let you know?" he asked.

"Yes," the man said. He let down the heavy ramp so David could pet the horse. "But let me know soon."

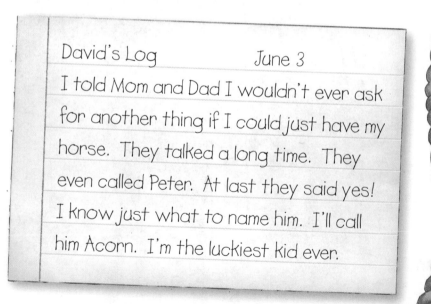

David's Log   June 3

I told Mom and Dad I wouldn't ever ask for another thing if I could just have my horse. They talked a long time. They even called Peter. At last they said yes! I know just what to name him. I'll call him Acorn. I'm the luckiest kid ever.

Acorn was young, only four. He was all brown but he had a white star on top of his nose. David loved the star best of all.

Although Acorn was a nice-looking horse, he was not a nice-acting horse. He was grumpy. He flashed his teeth a lot. He would raise up his back legs when David came near him. Everyone had to watch out. He was ready to kick even when someone was saying nice things to him.

David's Log   June 15

I don't think Acorn likes me—not even
a little bit. Jill says to give him time.
Dad says he won't let me keep a mean
horse, even if I want to. I don't mind
waiting for Acorn to get to know me.
I don't want to let him go.

Over and over again, David tried to win Acorn's trust. When he found out that horses like mint, he sprinkled mint over Acorn's food. When he found out that horses like sweets, David even gave him peaches to eat.

Although he tried to please Acorn, nothing seemed to help. Acorn was as grumpy as ever.

David's Log   June 23

Grandmother had a good idea! At dinner today, she said they got pets for their horses when she was a girl. Her father thought it helped them relax.

Who ever thought of that? A pet for a pet. I am going to get a pet for Acorn. I'll try anything!

Two days later, David found just the right pet for Acorn.

"Look, Acorn, I have a friend for you," said David. He put a kitten down over in a corner of Acorn's stall. Then he dashed to the side to watch. Would Acorn like the kitten being there?

Acorn walked over to the kitten. He didn't seem to mind her. He looked at the kitten. He sniffed her fur. He even pushed at her lightly with his nose. Then Acorn lifted his ears up.

David's Log   June 25

I named the kitten Tiger. She isn't even as big as one of Acorn's feet. I've been watching, and Acorn is being nice to Tiger. I hope his new pet will make him happy!

4 The Best Day Ever

David brushed and combed Acorn and played with the kitten every day. Acorn was very careful with Tiger. Although he was so much bigger than Tiger, he never stepped on the kitten with his heavy feet.

As the days went on, Acorn became more and more relaxed.

One day, Jill called David over and told him it was time to try walking Acorn. Acorn was great. He let David slip the halter over his head and he walked with him for over an hour.

David's Log   July 1

I gave Acorn a bath all by myself today!
Although he shook and even stamped
his feet, I could tell he liked it. I soaped
him and sprayed him over and over
again. The bath took over an hour. I
was soaked, but Acorn looked great.

"Now let's try the bridle and bit on Acorn," Jill grinned. "The bridle and bit are two items that go together. You need them to ride a horse. They help you tell the horse which way you want to go."

Although Acorn would not open up at first, he did take the bit in his mouth. Then David threw the saddle over his back. Acorn stood very still, even when David almost dropped the heavy saddle.

David's Log   July 10

The saddle is heavy, but I threw it over Acorn's back myself. I've been lifting it over and over so I can get used to how heavy it is.

After I got the saddle on Acorn, Jill let me get up on his back! Acorn was very relaxed. Now if only he will be that way when Dad comes to see him on Sunday!

Sunday was a big day for David—and for Acorn. David's family came over to the stable. Even his grandmother came.

Although Acorn had been so relaxed the last few days, David was not sure how he would act today. Would Acorn behave?

David climbed on the fence to put Acorn's bridle over his head. Acorn shook his head and stamped one foot.

"Are you all right, David?" his dad asked.

"Please," David whispered in Acorn's ear. The beautiful horse ducked his head and opened his mouth and let David slip the bit in. Then he stood still as David lifted the saddle into place.

Soon David was on Acorn's back.

"You look tall in the saddle!" said his grandmother.

David's Log   July 12
Today was the best day of my life! I hugged Acorn over and over when I took him back to the barn. I know that Acorn and I will be friends forever.

PHONICS

Decodable Words With the Phonic Elements

1 cv/cvc

begin	paper
clover	Peter
David	riders
frozen	student
layer	super
moment	tulips

2 cv/cvc

basin	Pilot
began	pupil
begin	Raven
Clover	relax
David	Rider
Jason	spider
label	student
Major	super
moment	Tulip
Music	

3 v/cvc

Acorn
even
over

4 v/cvc

Acorn
even
items
open
over